HOW THE GATOR'S SNOUT GREW OUT

© copyright 1998 by ARO Publishing.
Printed in the U.S.A. P.O. Box 193 Provo, Utah 84603

ISBN 0-89868-358-0–Library Bound
ISBN 0-89868-412-9–Soft Bound
ISBN 0-89868-359-9–Trade

A PREDICTABLE WORD BOOK

HOW THE GATOR'S SNOUT GREW OUT

Story by Janie Spaht Gill, Ph.D.
Illustrations by Bob Reese

 ARO PUBLISHING

Once a gator's snout looked like a pig's.

This is the tale of how his snout grew so big.

The wind was blowing one stormy day,

when the gator and the
muskrat went out
to play.

They played in the waves that floated in and out,

8

the muskrat was sitting on the gator's snout.

The rain came down, the
water rose high,

10

a log with holes came floating by.

The log jammed onto the gator's snout,

the gator pulled, but it wouldn't come out.

13

The gator tugged and tried to pull it out,

14

the muskrat helped tug at the
gator's snout.

They pushed and pulled and
tugged that snout,

18

they pushed and pulled, then
it finally popped out.

The gator's snout stretched out longer that day,

21

and that is the reason it looks this way.

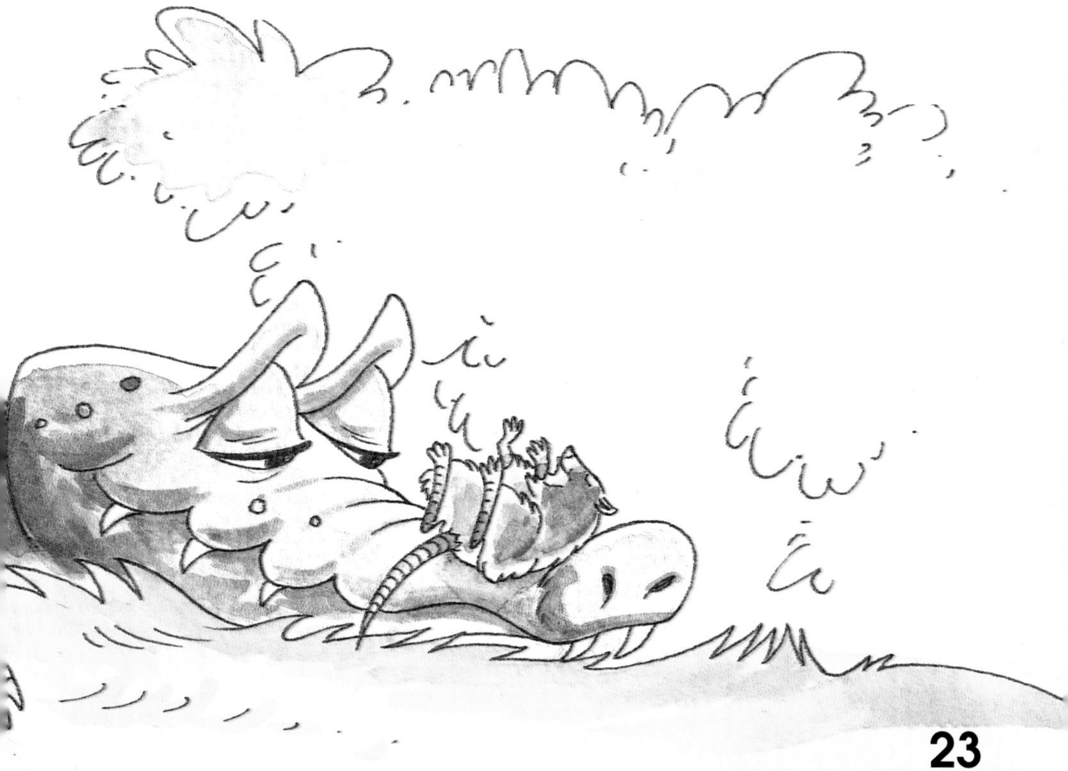

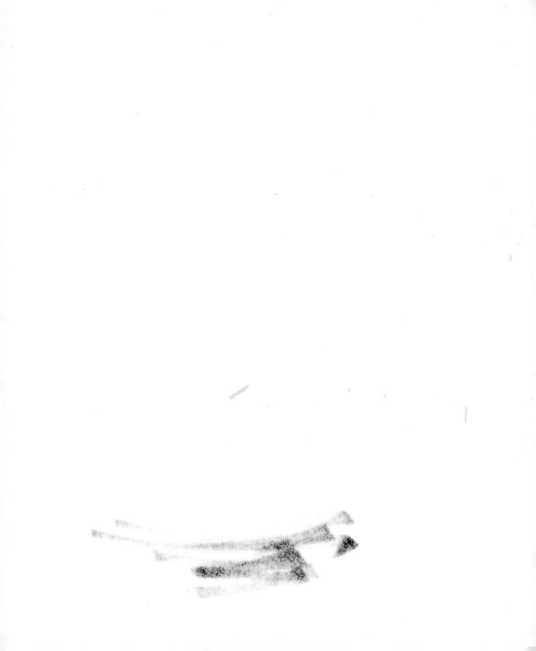